The Day We Said Goodbye to the Birds

Allan Dyen-Shapiro

Contents

Published in the United States of America by Rampant Loon Press, an imprint of Rampant Loon Media LLC, P.O. Box 111, Lake Elmo, Minnesota 55042. "Rampant Loon Press" and the Rampant Loon colophon are trademarks of Rampant Loon Media LLC.

www.rampantloonmedia.com

ISBN: 978-1-958333-18-1 (ebook)

ISBN: 978-1-958333-24-2 (print)

First Publication: June, 2025

Cover by 2Kool Studios

Background image © สมชัย ์พาลแก้ว / Adobe Stock

Foreground image © Dzmitry / Adobe Stock

Chapter One

Joe's eighteen-month-old daughter's hands clutched the seatback as she bounced up and down, blithely unaware of the reason for their escape from the San Francisco Bay Area. Unable to keep pace with the movement, her tie-dyed dress fluttered like a butterfly's wings. "Train," she said.

"Yes, Daphne. Train." Joe positioned his hand on her delicate shoulder. "We'll be in San Francisco soon."

She spun around and smiled at him. "Daphne Duck."

"Daphne Duck."

When she giggled, he kissed her forehead. Before her birth, when his wife had mentioned the name Daphne to his mother, Mom had worried the nickname, a feminization of Daffy, would emerge and scar Daphne for life. So far, no visible scarring.

On Daphne, at least. It was now ex-wife. Joe had scars.

"Blue line," the BART train announcer's voice intoned. The blue line would take them to the Transbay Transit Center in San Francisco, where they'd catch the bus for Oregon.

"Now departing Castro Valley."

The Oakland Hills fenced off this suburban haven, protecting it from poisonous breezes from San Francisco Bay. Joe couldn't have afforded the mortgage payments there on the salary paid by his job as a scientist for CyanoCorp, without his wife's earnings as a corporate lawyer.

Ex-wife. Ex-job.

At the next station, the train shuddered to a stop. "Bay Fair. Please put on protective gear. Position your mask first, then help any small children. Because of high toxin levels in the air today, at all aboveground stations, the doors will not open until compliance has been verified."

After molding the oblong, gray polyethylene over his nose and mouth, Joe adjusted the clear-plastic window of the eyepiece and fastened the Velcro straps.

"Daddy, funny."

With fingers spread into imaginary claws, he extended his arms toward her. "Aarrghh! Evil monster on the loose." He exaggerated the vocal distortion from the mask, hoping Daphne would find it goofy rather than disconcerting.

It worked—Daphne beamed and tittered.

Joe fished her mask from the container and encased her in less than three seconds. His proficiency stemmed from having consulted on testing the manufacturer's 2031 line of protective gear. He'd previously designed the anti-toxin-derivatized air filter the company had licensed for the masks, his last project before CyanoCorp had canned him in 2030.

In those days, he'd risen each morning entasked with a life mission—the world, his to save. These days, not so much.

"Thank you for wearing your anti-toxin mask. The doors will now open."

Many departing passengers wheeled suitcases; destination SFO, they'd escape via airplane. Armani suits pushed ahead, bound for San Francisco skyscrapers. Crocheted sweaters followed, headed to visit retirees in the Berkeley and Oakland Hills. Prevailing easterly winds spared most of the Bay Area from the toxin; the hills trapped it over the rest of Oakland.

Lowlanders entered, all black people. Short-lived gentrification at the turn of the century and a recent return of hipsters, artists, and apostles of impending revolution notwithstanding, these neighborhoods had been predominantly black since the 1940s. Most residents couldn't afford to leave their homes and had stayed. If they wore masks, most were fine, as it was primarily a respiratory toxin. Ocular and dermal lesions only afflicted those who routinely went out unprotected on high-toxin days.

The immunocompromised were more vulnerable, as were the elderly and the very young.

Daphne's eyes darted between these new passengers and the continuing ones. What differences did she notice? The tightly curled hair? The dark-colored skin?

The festering sores on the cheeks, foreheads, and hands of those wearing shabbier clothing? The economic downturn had forced many Oaklanders onto the streets where they were exposed twenty-four seven. Joe tried not to stare. He tried not to cry.

It was his fault.

Daphne chose a new friend. Just out of her arm's reach, this man leaned against a pole. He sported a tank top that flaunted his muscles, and he fingered a thick metal chain worn as a belt.

"Hi," she said. When she lifted her head to attempt eye contact, her hair brushed her shoulders.

Always the social butterfly. She didn't appear to notice the door closing or the train accelerating. Making friends took precedence. The man's eyes remained fixed on the ground.

"Hi. Daphne."

Startled, as if interrupted from a daydream, the man turned to Daphne and grinned. "Hey there. Daphne's a pretty name. You're a pretty girl. I'm Cassius."

"Cassius."

"That's right." He grasped the pole and knelt to her eye level. "You're a smart girl, too."

"You got kids?" Joe asked.

Cassius planted his hand on the seatback and pushed himself to a standing position. In a whisper, as if he didn't want Daphne to hear, he answered. "Three. Had four, but Lavinia died from the toxin. Just last month. Two weeks after her third birthday. The sores had already blinded her..."

"I'm sorry," Joe said.

As he showed no sign of identifying Joe—and how could he have, with Joe's face hidden behind the mask?—Cassius couldn't realize Joe's apology was more than empathy. Anonymity offered safety.

Or not. A diminutive old man in a plaid shirt who sat three rows behind Joe must have recognized Joe's voice despite the mask muffling it—he waved. "Hey, Joe. How you been? Just noticed you there."

So much for anonymity. Joe turned and spoke across empty seats. "Okay. And you?" A delay tactic. The twenty seconds it bought allowed him to place the voice behind the mask: Adam Jackson. A janitor, he worked for the cleaning company Cyano-Corp had contracted.

The silence ended with Adam exhaling deliberately. "You heard about Trudy?"

"Yeah. My ex-wife saw the obituary. I'm sorry. I would have gone to the funeral, but..."

Adam smirked and shook his head. "That'd been a fool thing to do. You know damn well it would've turned ugly. I was sad enough—you wanted to start a brawl and have more folks get hurt? She died from toxin inhalation. Your toxin."

Cassius's attention drifted from Daphne to Joe. He eyeballed Joe as if straining to make a mental connection. Exploring, calculating, he was a sevengill shark—the Bay's top predator—contemplating a potential meal.

"San Leandro station," the recorded voice announced.

Walking backward without breaking eye contact, Cassius stepped toward the door.

"Bye-bye, Cassius." Daphne extended and retracted her tiny fingers.

"Bye, baby girl." Cassius shrugged his shoulders and exited, along with several other passengers.

For a moment, Joe closed his eyes and sank into the cushion.

Adam leaned his forearms on the seat and narrowed the distance between his mask and Joe's. "Sorry. I wasn't thinking. We can talk now—there's nobody else in the car."

Moisture blurred Joe's vision. He peered through the window at a train passing in the opposite direction on the adjacent tracks: a swish pan in soft focus, like the memories replaying in his head.

Adam's voice dropped several steps in pitch. "I didn't mean to upset you, Joe. You got a bum rap. I'm just old and sad."

Joe was sad, too, but Adam wasn't responsible. "It might as well have been my toxin. I'm not innocent. I screwed up." Without averting his eyes from the window, Joe stretched his right leg to relieve a cramp and repositioned Daphne. With a yawn, she rested her head against Joe's shirt.

"I don't blame you, but a lot of this city does. Someone would have beaten the shit out of you if you'd come. Trudy's in Heaven. I'm sure she understands."

Joe switched Daphne to his left arm, so he could cross

himself with his right. Although he hadn't been in a church in a decade and hadn't prayed in longer, the ritual had stuck with him. In times calling for reverence, he defaulted to it.

"Love that Catholic thing," Adam said.

Adam's growly laugh cast away some of Joe's world-weariness. "Habit. No God would let us do what we did to San Francisco Bay—"

"Now don't you go blaspheming. I always liked you, and your daughter is a treasure, but if you're going to insult my God, I'll sit somewhere else."

"Sorry." Joe's pro forma, performative use of this word had become punctuation, but still, he meant it.

Daphne slept. Joe looked at his watch—naptime.

Apology apparently accepted, Adam settled into his seat. After loosening his mask, he coughed into a handkerchief. Adam straightened his old-man cap and readjusted the Velcro straps that held his mask in place. A few minutes later, he stood and took the seat beside Joe. His voice sank to a whisper as if they were co-conspirators. "Friends expect me to be some kind of expert since I worked at CyanoCorp. I tell them I know a lot about their toilets but not much about the bacteria."

With a lapse into lecture mode, Joe described horizontal evolution for the millionth time. The cyanobacteria had picked up the toxin gene from another microbe in the environment.

As if listening to a preacher, Adam nodded rhythmically. He laid his hand on Joe's. "I told everyone it wasn't your fault. You didn't do it." With his other hand, he caught the seat, steadying himself. "Natural stuff. Bad luck, that's all, I said. Nobody bought it. Too easy to blame you."

Blaming Joe had worked for CyanoCorp, for the Senator who had gotten them an EPA appropriation to fund the R&D, and for the Governor who had approved the contract to deploy the system.

Adam pivoted and pointed toward the opposite window. "Here's your nickname in this neighborhood."

It was spray-painted on the sound barrier: *Genocide Joe*. A few dozen feet further, *Die, white boy!* Nothing Joe hadn't seen on TV footage, although the absence of profanity was atypical.

When Joe peeled himself from the seatback, the air conditioning chilled his skin where he'd perspired through his shirt. "You think they like me any better in Castro Valley?"

"I wouldn't advise getting off in Oakland. And even in San Francisco, you better be going to a patrolled zone."

"We'll stay in the bus terminal," Joe said. "And I'll keep the mask on."

"Where you going?"

"Eugene. I have family there. We can stay with them until I'm back on my feet. After the divorce, I'm too depressed to sell myself to a new employer." Joe leaned into the seat. Breath vented through his pursed lips.

"I seen you'd lost a few pounds and let your hair go scraggly."

It was that noticeable? "I want to lie on a bed and shut out the world. At least for a few weeks. My cousin's kids adore Daphne and will keep her busy. Eventually, someone will hire me—my name's less toxic the further I get from here. Greyhound bus leaves from the Transit Center."

"Bus? What about the Lexus?"

"Wife took it in the divorce." Besides, he'd been too distracted to feel safe about driving so far. CyanoCorp's testimony had landed him on a no-fly list, so the bus was the best option.

Adam shook his head. "Didn't spend enough to get a good lawyer? Oh yeah, your wife, she is a lawyer. They protect their own."

"I got what I wanted."

His eyes twinkled. "You kept the house. Good man."

Joe's gaze met Adam's. "No, the realtor's putting our home up for sale. I finished prepping it and gave up the keys today." The house had too many reminders of 'Genocide Joe.' His wife had loved him once, but no woman would relish being a monster's wife. Joe understood her need for a clean break and bore her no ill will.

The wrinkles on Adam's forehead deepened. "Let me wrap my head around this. Your ex has the car. You had to do the scut work around the house even though she'll pocket half the money from it." He raised an eyebrow. "And you got what you wanted? What reminded her so much of you that she didn't want it?"

Joe nodded toward Daphne, who slept on his arm.

A look of horror on his face, the old man ran his hand through Daphne's hair.

Chapter Two

Adam departed at the Coliseum, and Joe wished him well.

Two stations later, the train stopped. "All passengers must exit. Due to electrical problems, the blue line terminates today at Lake Merritt. Please exit the station and board a shuttle bus for West Oakland."

Oakland. Crap. Adam's warning reverberated in Joe's head.

The mask would hide him. He hoped.

Hands shaking, Joe unfolded the umbrella stroller. Daphne had chosen it; she'd fingered the black and orange bird with the big eyes as her "namesake." Joe set his still-sleeping child in the seat. Click went the buckle.

Joe snaked his arms through the straps of the backpack he'd procured for his honeymoon in the Swiss Alps. Two zippered bags clipped to the external frame. One contained diapers and baby wipes; the other held plastic cups, purified water, and small boxes of Cheerios.

The doors receded. Joe angled Daphne's stroller to lift the wheels over the gap.

Upon waking up, Daphne spied a poster advertising the estuary at Lake Merritt. Her favorite locale, home of the birds, and she knew it. Joe hadn't accompanied her in over a year, but she'd visited frequently with her babysitter on low-toxin days. "Daddy. Birds. Birds."

"No birds, kiddo. We're in the BART station." The subterranean cavern had excluded them, even when winged creatures had been plentiful. "Birds don't live in subway stations."

She disagreed. "Bird. Bird."

Her finger pointed to a man with hands and face greased white by mime's makeup. He contorted his arms and flapped them.

"Funny. Funny."

Playing to his audience, the man swooped bench to bench. Lips to the cement, he pantomimed sucking a worm. Daphne laughed and laughed, fogging her mask.

As he finished "digesting" the worm, he froze, no doubt expecting a tip. When Joe extracted his wallet from his pocket, the mime lunged, snagged it, and mouthed the words "thank you." His back to Joe, he dashed off, swinging his elbows high.

Panicking, Joe tried to reach for it, but each time, the mime deftly avoided his fingers.

With what cash the mime found lifted above his head, he danced away from Joe again and then held up the bus tickets. To the crowd, all was fun and games until he found Joe's driver's license. His eyes met Joe's with an icy glower. He returned the contents to the wallet and handed it back.

His act continued: the "ground" that had yielded a worm now provided water. His sips slowed. He scrambled in the direction of the bench and hopped on. For a second, his body was frozen. It convulsed. His pantomimed flight zigzagged as he fought to stay airborne. He fell to the ground.

Daphne no longer laughed.

When the mime opened his eyes and mouthed Joe's name, Joe ran, pushing the stroller as fast as he could, escaping toward the escalator at the other end of the platform. After wheeling the stroller onto the moving stairs, Joe looked over his shoulder. The mime lay motionless, but his eyes hadn't left them.

A crowd also stared.

Joe's knees buckled, and he flailed for the railing to steady himself. He and Daphne reached the top, where he let go and took a tentative step forward.

"Walk, Daddy."

Finding an attendant to open the gate would have delayed them, so Joe acquiesced. Once free, Daphne bounded out of the stroller. Joe took her hand, and with his other hand, executed the one-handed stroller-folding maneuver every parent learns.

"Please don protective gear before traversing the airlock," an automated voice said. Downtown Oakland stations were below ground and circulated filtered air, so most passengers had taken their masks off. Joe and Daphne hadn't.

Once through the turnstiles, they emerged into a semicircular fishbowl ringed with metal. The floor smelled of urine; Daphne turned up her nose. Air whooshed, and doors closed behind them. A click confirmed they were free from the mime but trapped with six others from the crowd. Joe stood in silence, stomach rock hard and chest tight, until the opposite doors opened, revealing a staircase to street level. The other passengers dispersed.

One-by-one, Daphne ascended the steps. Her pink-sneakered left foot went first; the right followed.

Too slow. Joe scooped Daphne up and carried her. At the top, he unfolded the stroller, and she bounced back in.

They exited onto Oak Street and into a police officer's surveillance. His eyes followed them.

A beefy man with a paunch that strained his belt, the cop's unkempt beard extended beyond the bounds of his mask. "You here for the festival?" His fingers massaged his gun.

"No. Just to catch the shuttle bus."

"Stay. It's important for you Hill folks to see us Lowlanders. Otherwise, you forget we exist. I want Hill folks to feel safe and enjoy themselves when they in my neighborhood."

It didn't seem wise to volunteer that he lived beyond the Hills. Used to.

The cop took his hand off the gun and scratched below his mask. "I volunteered for duty today. This is my home, and I want the festival to succeed, and so does every local cop I know. The state troopers they brought in as re-enforcements—" he shook his head. "Let's just say they're not as comfortable with the people who live here."

The state had set up a Special Toxic Zone Unit to protect property. Most owners of this property lived outside Oakland.

Down the street, a station employee directed transit riders toward a bus with the BART logo. Beside the bus, four unmasked black men conversed. They passed a cell phone one to the other.

Their lips mouthed Joe's name. The cell phone must have had an ID device. Weren't those illegal?

Oblivious, Daphne fiddled with the straps of her stroller.

Joe stuck close to the police officer. "Maybe we will check the festival out. What's going on?" As stealthily as possible, Joe snuck a hand into his pocket and turned off his cell—no more tracking his whereabouts.

The man's shoulders relaxed. "Oakland Peace Festival. First time since the catastrophe. Poetry slam, music, dancers, carnival rides, games for the kids. The usual political crap, but you can ignore all that. And food. You white folks don't get much soul food up there in the Hills. Bet you haven't eaten Oakland-style barbecue in years."

Joe hadn't—not worth toxin exposure or risking recognition for take-out. "I'm partial to Grandma's Chicken and Ribs. Are they going to be there?"

"You bet." The man rubbed his belly. "My favorite, too. Best sauce in the world."

Joe's stomach rumbled. "Daphne's never tasted their sweet potato pie."

"Lord, have mercy. You got to get the child a piece of pie."

The bus pulled away. From the windows, the men gawked and pointed at Joe.

"Will do. Wave bye-bye to the nice man, Daphne."

Daphne blew him a kiss. He returned it.

The cop's suggestion appealed. Better than waiting around for the next bus—those guys would have friends. With Joe's cell off, they couldn't track a moving target. And Joe couldn't call a taxi without using his cell, so he didn't have a better option. On the slim chance someone at the festival would know what Joe looked like, the mask would hide him. Later in the day, he and Daphne could walk to a different BART station.

Daphne could visit the birds one last time before they left the Bay Area.

Chapter Three

Decision made, they set off at a brisk pace. Daphne sat quietly, taking in the scenery. Five quick blocks took them past the long-shuttered Oakland Public Library building. Ahead, Lake Merritt sparkled with blue-green streaks embedded in a darker brown-green: cyanobacteria. The wrecked sign that proclaimed Lake Chalet Seafood Bar and Grill, Joe's former favorite lunch spot, taunted him. *Where have you been? Oh yeah, you only came here with your now ex-wife. Before you destroyed the entire town.*

Joe commanded the voices to stop. Usually, they plagued only his nights, but he'd slipped into a daydream. Was it too much to ask to enjoy a day with his daughter?

One voice knew his name. "Joe, is that you?"

This one wasn't a phantom. The words had bubbled up from the lake. Curious, Joe approached.

"I'll meet you on the pier," a man in a boat said. A full headshield, clear plastic around the eyes, extended down to his neck where it met a rubber bodysuit. Gloves and boots completed his entombment.

To reach the man, Joe wheeled Daphne through the ruins of the restaurant. She squirmed, wanting out of the stroller.

The man paddled up beside them. "Don't come any closer. You're not dressed for it. Toxin is too concentrated." He hefted a box filled with slime onto the dock where patio furniture used to sit and emptied the gelatinous contents.

"You don't recognize my voice, do you?"

Not through the headgear.

It hit him. "Vishva Ray?"

"Yeah, man. How you been? I'd hug you, but you wouldn't want cyanocrap on you."

When Vishva turned to look into the stroller, Daphne waved.

"She's so big! But she still has those pretty eyes. I haven't seen her since she was two months old. When you had us over for dinner at your house. Remember?"

"Sure. But why are you out there in a boat?"

He paused, contemplating his answer. "Why aren't *you* out here?"

His rejoinder jogged Joe's memory; he'd read about Vishva's efforts. Vishva could only skim the scum, but it sufficed to spare the birds. Avian life was sensitive to the toxin. Lake Merritt Estuary survived thanks to Joe's former technician.

Joe didn't respond.

"Well," Vishva said, "for me, it is dharma. I overexpressed the gas vesicle gene. These buggers wouldn't float at the top if I hadn't done my job. You were proud of me when I showed you them under the microscope—so many vesicles they looked black. You wanted them jumping out of the water." He extended his arm toward the lake as if to show Joe his handiwork. "They do jump—enough for me to scoop them up. They grow back, but I stay ahead of it. The birds live. At least in my corner of Oakland."

"Do the locals give you any trouble?"

A sigh segued into a polite chortle. "To them, I'm the crazy Indian guy. I don't dare reveal I was Genocide Joe's technician."

His words cut. Wounds festered in silence.

Joe's old friend proffered what he likely thought a salve. "Joe, why don't you join me? Perhaps, it is your dharma, too?"

"We're leaving for Eugene. Tonight." And even if they weren't, he was too recognizable. He couldn't fly under the radar screen like Vishva did.

Vishva's shoulders slumped. "My wife would have been thrilled to have you and Daphne at our home for dinner."

Joe's belly hungered for Vishva's wife's lentil soup.

"Next time, okay?"

If there was a next time. Joe managed a polite nod.

"What will you do in Eugene?"

A difficult question to answer. If Joe's life were a run on the *Line Rider* game he'd played as a child, the roller coaster would have ended in mid-air, with no continuing tracks in sight. "Anything other than genetic engineering of cyanobacteria."

Vishva's silence suggested disapproval; his advice that followed confirmed it. "You cannot run from your dharma." His sad voice conveyed empathy in four simple words: "Be well, my friend."

"You too, Vishva." *Seriously?* Vishva thought Joe should go back to working with cyanobacteria? Joe's name was poison—nobody would let him. And even if they would, he was out of ideas.

Joe pivoted Daphne around but halted in response to Vishva's urgent call. "Wait. Take my spare headshield. You will get killed if someone recognizes you."

"No, thanks," Joe said. "I'll roast in it."

"Joe, I'll reincarnate as a cockroach if I don't talk some

sense into you. If it were just you, I'd say let the insane bastard do as he wishes. But you need to wear it for Daphne's sake."

Frisbee-style, he launched the package toward Joe. Joe caught it one-handed under his lifted leg.

Vishva cackled. "When you get to Eugene, buy a house with a yard. I'll visit and organize the Ultimate Frisbee game at your next barbecue. Now, put the damn thing on while I'm watching you. I'm not going back to scooping the green crap until I know you'll be safe."

The straps pinched under Joe's ear; the back of his neck itched. Salty perspiration attacked his sensitive skin. "Thanks. I'll email when I get to Eugene."

"Siddhartha returns to work. So long, Joe."

After waving goodbye, Joe wheeled Daphne back onto Lakeside Drive. They followed it around the water until it dead-ended into Harrison Street. With a squeal, Daphne registered a complaint; Joe found a bench and broke out the changing mat and a fresh diaper.

No other humans crossed their path until Harrison led them to Grand Avenue, the main drag in this part of Oakland. When she saw people, Daphne sat up in the stroller.

Addicts—bodies shaking, eyes vacant—wandered in every direction. One thrust a cup in Joe's face. "Please, Sir, spare change."

"No. Sorry. Baby girl. Got to go." Joe sped up until the pedestrian crowd no longer consisted of panhandlers.

"Hi," Daphne called to every passer-by. When one waved, Daphne giggled.

When they reached Perkins Street, Joe turned off Grand, losing the crowd. His pulse slowed, but his face itched, and his skin sizzled. Thinking them alone, he took off his headgear and Daphne's too, unbuttoned his shirt, and wiped his brow with the sleeve.

"Better button up—high toxin level today."

The unexpected words from behind Joe set his heart racing. He nearly jumped.

"Good thing you got a long-sleeve shirt. But why's your facial protection in your hand, not on your head?" The speaker's voice marked her as female, young, and black. Her full headshield and rubber body suit prevented further identification.

"I guess I didn't listen to the radio," Joe said.

"Well, that's dumb. And your baby girl—you want her all scabby?" The woman's eyes focused on Joe's Harvard logo shirt. "You dress like you got an education—why you acting stupid?"

"I'm sorry—"

"Yes, you are one sorry excuse for a father." She unfolded a clear plastic mesh. Magnets clamped it to the handles of Daphne's stroller and again at the base. "There, now. She's all protected. Anti-toxin netting—it screens out air pollutants, too. Our cooperative developed these for when a mask isn't enough. I wouldn't have a baby out here for more than an hour without one. You've never seen them?"

Joe was curious. "Where did you get the anti-toxin?"

"CyanoCorp offered it. We protested outside their headquarters until they did. And their top surface chemist quit and came to work with us."

Christina Riederer. With her youth spent distributing Marxist propaganda and tussling with German cops, Joe could envision her bailing on corporate America.

"She's my hero. She made the fat cats back down. So, I'm here with these nets. I used to teach in a preschool—it closed when the companies near it left. This keeps me around children. I'd missed them." Her voice adopted a commanding tone. "You too, headshield on."

Joe complied.

Hand atop Daphne's stroller, the woman knelt down. "Hi, there."

"Hi."

"You're a beautiful girl. What's your name?"

"Daphne Duck."

The woman snickered. "I bet you like ducks. There are lots of them here. They're beautiful, too. You like all sorts of birds?"

"Birds. Birds. Birds."

"You've made a friend," Joe said. "You have common interests."

"Yeah, my daughter loved the estuary too. She died. Genocide Joe's toxin."

"That's awful." Joe suppressed the urge to say he was sorry.

"Walk with me," she said. "You can't keep Daphne away from the birds. She's jumping out of her skin."

After one block, Perkins crossed Bellevue Avenue. They ambled the short distance past dying trees and rusted park benches to the estuary proper. As Daphne caught sight of the five islands ahead of them, she strained against the belt.

"Let me help you." The woman unbuckled the stroller straps and wrapped Daphne in the net, sealing it with the magnets. "A cocoon for my butterfly." She laid Daphne in Joe's arms and extended her hand. "Kiara."

From underneath Daphne, Joe wriggled his hand free, but he avoided offering his name.

Unsuccessfully.

"And you are? I could call you Daphne's Daddy, but I prefer to address folks with their Christian names."

What to call himself? Joe settled on his middle name. "Steve."

"Well, Steve, I want to thank you for bringing your daughter down from the Hills today. How long you been living out there?" As Kiara spoke, she unzipped her purse and reached in.

"Ten years. Ever since I finished my Ph.D. My wife's parents covered the down payment on a house. And you? Are you native to the Bay Area?"

Kiara whipped out her cell phone and pressed a button. "You hesitated too long in coming up with 'Steve.' I'm hoping it's because you're a famous actor trying to stay incognito, but lots of child predators hang around here. I've been recording you—the FBI voice recognition app should just take a second..."

Her face froze.

She'd identified him. Shit. His pulse quickened, pounding beneath his temples.

"Genocide Joe? You the guy who's responsible for this mess?" She dialed.

"I didn't mean to do it. I was trying to save San Francisco Bay." Unsure whether to negotiate or flee and not wanting to tip his hand, Joe surveyed escape routes.

"Well, you messed up big time, Joe."

"I know."

She spoke into the phone. "By the Lake. Genocide Joe." With her thumb, she disconnected the call. "You got ten minutes to live, asshole."

Chapter Four

Anticipating the direction from which the assassin would approach was impossible, as was outrunning him while pushing a stroller. This woman wouldn't kill Daphne—or would she? And even if she wouldn't, what would become of his child? Joe shuddered involuntarily, held his breath.

The woman's eyes swept Joe head to toe and back. "I imagined horns and a tail. You don't seem evil." She rested her foot on a bench and rubbed her leg. "Sores itch."

"Sorry." Could he talk his way out of this? He struggled to dampen his fight-or-flight edginess, to calm his racing thoughts, to listen for cues to guide him in pleading his case.

Joe's apology elicited an eye roll and a long exhale. "You brought that get-up for hiding. When I caught you, why didn't you pretend you had a gun? It might have worked."

While biting his upper lip, Joe attempted to formulate an answer. "I'm not a good liar."

"No wonder corporate America fired your ass." She whispered as if to keep her thoughts from Daphne. "I've dreamed about killing you. I bought a Glock off a dealer; my husband's gonna bring it. No use running—I'll yell, and someone else will get the satisfaction. Your toxin killed my daughter. Ripped the inside of her lungs out. You know what it's like to see your baby girl in a pool of her own blood? Screaming, and then not screaming?"

All Joe could do was shake his head.

"You're pathetic. Showing up here with your daughter, looking like a nice, average guy." She rolled her neck, cracking it. Eyes in Joe's direction, accusing, she crossed her arms. "Why'd you do it? What do you mean you were trying to save the Bay?"

The Internet had circulated misinformation, and hackers had blocked CyanoCorp's website. Time running out, Joe decided to give Kiara the abbreviated version. "The Bay was getting salty. Agriculture, industry, and the cities all drew off too much freshwater. Everything was dying. My group made cyanobacteria capture moisture from fog. I'd thought we'd be heroes, but it picked up a toxin from another bug and added a lipid that made the toxin volatile."

Kiara planted her feet in a wide stance and clenched her fists. "You're talking to me like I'm ten years old. I'm not stupid. I got a degree from Cal—I took a few science courses. Tell me how cyanobacteria were supposed to squeeze water out of fog."

No longer the center of attention for either adult, Daphne fidgeted.

"We'll see the birds in a second, kiddo." If Daddy could talk his way out of an execution.

Joe's focus returned to Kiara. "Water channels. Most are holes in a cell membrane, so they lack directionality. I started with bacteriorhodopsin—a pump evolved to push protons. I played with the central part, designing a pore big enough for a water molecule. It worked. It pushed water molecules."

Kiara's eyes fixed on Joe's. "Go on."

She could have Googled for what Joe was telling her. Was she looking for an excuse not to hurt him? A way to make sense out of her daughter's death?

Joe explained how he'd fused the DNA for the water pump to an adhesion domain to make multiple copies of the pump stick together. When he expressed it in cyanobacteria, the pumps clumped in the membrane and attached to an internal structure at the bottom of the cells.

"So, the bottom expels water into the Bay, and the top sticks out into the foggy air and replaces it. The readings showed our strategy was working." Well, it was up to the point when they stopped taking readings. When children started dying. "You get any of this?"

"Enough. You didn't intend to kill my daughter."

The accusation reduced from murder to manslaughter, Joe exhaled. His adrenaline surge began to abate.

"But if you were a righteous white dude, why science? Why didn't you organize and get the rich bastards to stop using so much water?"

Because he wouldn't have gotten the elegant house in Castro Valley? Because politics was less of an intellectual challenge?

"Science was what I knew. It was my way to serve man."

While shuffling her feet, she looked down at Joe's. "Twilight Zone fan?"

The reference elicited a chuckle.

"Stop laughing. You aren't my friend. You still killed my daughter, even if you didn't mean to."

Kiara got out her cell phone and held it while she glowered at Joe. When Daphne smiled at her, she dialed. "False alarm. Wasn't him. Sorry."

New arrivals obviated further discussion. "I see another

dumb-ass white family abusing their kid. I got to go talk sense into them. Keep hiding behind your get-up—just because I'm willing to let you live doesn't mean everyone here is."

Away she strode, but after a few paces, she turned and spoke in a halting voice that held back tears. "Your daughter's adorable. Take care of her. And if you think science can help, do your best to get us out of this mess. Okay?"

"Absolutely." It seemed unwise to convey doubt as to his abilities.

She left them.

Left Joe shaken, but in better spirits than he'd been in months.

Left Joe with a mission: to get Kiara, to get Oakland, to get the entire Bay out of this mess.

Left Joe wondering—was his dharma, to use Vishva's word, to keep working on a solution to the toxin problem? If so, how? No, his promise to Kiara was empty. He didn't want it to be—it would be fantastic to merit the epithet *righteous white dude*. But he didn't deserve it.

Was there another way to deserve it?

He'd promised his daughter birds—that promise he could keep. He pivoted Daphne into a front-facing carry and ambled the few dozen meters to the edge of Lake Merritt.

"Birds. Birds. Birds." Like a caterpillar soon to emerge from its cocoon, Daphne struggled within the net.

His awareness of the necessity for caution heightened, Joe suffered beneath Vishva's headshield and was soon steam-cooked to a fatigue that barely allowed him to hold Daphne. Half an hour of toxin exposure couldn't harm her. With nobody around, he undid the magnets. It couldn't hurt him much either, so he jettisoned his facial protection.

A huge smile on her face, Daphne raced to the fence and latched on. Her eyes followed the descent of a great egret.

When it landed on one of the man-made islands, Daphne clapped. Her attention returned to the sky.

"It was an egret," Joe said.

"Bird," she corrected.

"Okay, bird." Joe guffawed and tried again. "Look over there on the rock, Daphne. Follow my finger." She did. "This is a cormorant. She's drying off her wings. She was fishing, and she got wet. She can't fly until she's dry again. Can you say *cormorant?*"

Daphne obliged as best she could. "More-mant."

"Cormorant," Joe repeated.

"Daddy bird."

"Okay, Daddy's bird. I do like them. Do you like cormorants, Daphne?"

She might have answered, but just then, she spied her favorites. "Duck, duck."

"You're right. Those are Mallard ducks."

"Daphne Duck."

"No, you're Daphne Duck. Those are Mallard ducks."

"Bird." She radiated pride at having won the argument. She'd make a great lawyer. Took after her mom.

"My favorite are the black-crowned night herons," a voice from behind them said.

Joe tripped over the stroller and scrambled to put his head-shield back on.

"Sorry, I didn't mean to startle you."

"Ni-herun," Daphne said.

Her attention captured, the twenty-something woman locked eyes with Daphne. "You're right, darling. There's a night heron over there. It's hunting. Oh, it will settle for frogs or insects or other yucky stuff. But it likes fish better. If you watch, I bet it will catch one. Look."

Daphne's eyes tracked the young woman's fingers and

focused on the bird. Sure enough, it plucked a fish from the water and gobbled it. Daphne waved her arms excitedly.

"She's cute." The woman twiddled a surgical steel chain stretched between piercings of her cheek and ear. The chain matched another that connected the pocket and zipper of her torn black jeans. An unbuttoned leather jacket framed a T-shirt emblazoned with the slogan, *All the Cute Girls are Lesbians.*

"You here for the festival? It's starting soon. I'm working it for Punk Voter—we're going to take control of Oakland away from the fat cats. Are you registered?"

"I don't live in Oakland," Joe said.

She opened a gym bag to reveal clipboards. "It's okay. I live in Berkeley myself. I can still get you registered. Where do you live?"

"Castro Valley."

"Oh," she said, her expression changing to disgust. "You are a fat cat."

Although Joe stepped back, creating distance, his eyes kept focus on hers. "Maybe once. Wife divorced me. I don't live anywhere anymore—Daphne and I are leaving town today. Eugene, Oregon, will be our new home."

Appearing satisfied with Joe's explanation, she put down her bag. "My partner grew up in Eugene. She's at the festival, attending to her booth. Piercings are her side job. She did mine —you like them?"

"Pretty," Daphne said.

The woman knelt close. "Oh, you like them. You are so sweet. I want to have a daughter like you someday."

As if on cue, Daphne kissed her. She reached for the woman's chain. An anticipated move: the woman caught Daphne's hand and kissed it.

"Can I hold her?"

"Of course," Joe said.

She raised Daphne in the air and shook her while making clown faces and silly noises.

"She wants to be held upside down," Joe said. "It's her favorite way to play."

"Glad you told me. I wouldn't want to drop her."

A monkey, Daphne somersaulted in the woman's arms, hung with hair touching the ground—arms akimbo—and giggled. Also smiling, the woman pressed her hand against Daphne's neck, rotating Daphne to her feet.

"Again," Daphne said.

"I'd love to play with you all day, but I have to go to work. Got to go make new friends and tell them to vote."

Upon hearing the word "vote," two young women with dog collars around their necks and ripped T-shirts took in Sunshine's clipboards and darted in the opposite direction, holding hands and giggling. A man with a salt-and-pepper beard and dreadlocks peeking out of a crocheted cap gave Sunshine the finger. A state trooper looked around, whispered something into a walkie-talkie, and decided to follow the Rasta.

"Vote," Daphne said.

When Joe nabbed Daphne from behind and plopped her into the stroller, her attention remained with the woman.

"I should bring you along. I bet nobody would argue with you." The woman continued in a muffled voice. "Nobody would tell me to get my white butt out of their business."

"So, you've gotten some of that today, too." Joe corralled Daphne to prevent her from sliding out of the stroller.

"Every day. But it's what the festival is about. Divided, we can be controlled. United, we can fix anything. When folks realize this, we'll clean up the Bay, put people back to work, and get rid of the damn toxin."

If only it was so easy.

"Eat," Daphne said.

"Is she hungry? There are vendors over at Lakeside Park. My partner's vegan, but festivals are one of the few times I can eat meat without her getting on my case. I tell her I'm being culturally sensitive—actually, I just like ribs. Walk with me— I'm going that way."

Daphne reached her arms toward the woman.

"Okay, precious. I'll carry you if it's all right with your dad."

When Joe nodded and loosened his grip, Daphne leaped into the woman's arms. Joe lagged a few steps behind and pushed the stroller.

"I didn't catch your name. Mine's Sunshine Love—I made it up. My partner will take my last name when we get married."

"My name's Larry." No equivocation in Joe's voice—he'd learned his lesson.

She transferred Daphne to the other shoulder. Wide-eyed, Daphne surveyed the crowd, which thickened as they approached the festival.

"So, does your ex share custody with you? Is it Daddy's day with the kid?"

"Every day is Daddy's day. I have full custody."

A stunned expression captured Sunshine's face, and she froze in her tracks. "Are you serious? Your ex gave up this gorgeous baby? Next, you're going to tell me she's an investment banker, right?"

"Lawyer."

"That was my second guess." Sunshine looked Daphne right in the eye. "My mother told me not to share my life with someone who won't commit. Right now, you got your daddy behind you. He's a nice man. He loves you. Don't settle for anything less, ever."

Daphne's gaze matched Sunshine's for intensity and seriousness. When Sunshine stopped speaking, Daphne leaned forward and kissed the un-pierced cheek.

With much effort, Joe restrained himself from doing the same. Few women took his side with such conviction when divorce was mentioned.

"You should put her back in the toxin net," Sunshine said. "I like to go without it too—it makes me feel human. But she's gotten max exposure for a baby."

Sunshine handed her back. "It was wonderful meeting you. You two are beautiful people. My partner's going to hate you, though. She's in for some when-are-we-going-to-have-a-baby nagging tonight."

"It was a pleasure." Joe meant it. Normal human interaction. He netted Daphne back into her stroller.

"Bye-bye," Daphne said.

"Bye, pretty girl. Peace." Sunshine walked away.

Despite the discomfort from the head shield, Joe pushed the stroller with an extra spring in his steps. Could he put his funk behind him and do something productive? Maybe joblessness would enable exploration of solutions to the mess he'd caused. Maybe he'd park himself in the U. of O. library once he hit Eugene and brainstorm. Maybe he should—

"Eeeeaaaat!" Daphne's guttural roar announced the advent of lunchtime.

"I take it you're hungry. Wiping barbecue sauce off the stroller could get icky, so we'll do Asian. Chicken and rice sound good?"

"Mmmmmm."

At the first food vendor they encountered, Joe purchased lemongrass chicken over rice and requested an extra Styrofoam bowl. He forked some over for Daphne and thrust her portion under the net. She grabbed a handful of rice and shoved it in her mouth. To allow eating but still hide his identity, Joe loosened the straps on his protective gear.

A public address system broke through the din of the crowd and belted out its distorted message. "Poetry slam begins at eleven A.M. in Area A."

"Let's go. We can chow down while Daddy listens to the poets."

Occupied with her lunch, Daphne continued chewing.

A welcome breeze cooled Joe as they strolled along a dirt path to a grove secluded on one side by trees and on the other by the backs of festival tents. Upon reaching a sprawling oak tree, Joe set the stroller's parking brake. The partial shade was the best he could do. "Daddy's going to sit down next to you and finish his lunch."

The only person on stage in a jacket and tie, presumably the emcee, approached the microphone. "Check, check. Can you all hear me?"

The crowd answered with applause.

"Welcome to the Oakland Peace Festival. I want to give a shout-out to my mother, who came down from the Hills for the day, and any other Hill folk out there. We Lowlanders need your support to take Oakland back for the people. Let's hear it for the Hill folks."

Applause again; it was polite but underwhelming.

"Today, we got a treat for you all. Just in from LA, this man is the poet laureate of Echo Park—Ground Zero for the Re-Mexicanization of the Southland campaign. White folks stole the land from brown folks back in 1848, and they didn't get it back for almost two centuries. It's a bit long to wait, but we black folks still have something to learn from them. So, let's welcome the teacher, the preacher, the LA creature: Señor Paco Hernandez."

A diminutive fellow in workman's overalls and a T-shirt

that read "F*** the cops" took the stage and grabbed the mic from the emcee. "*Hola*, Oakland. *¿Cómo están ustedes?*"

Boisterous cheering answered his question. As it began to fade out, synthesized percussion blasted an assault on the eardrums while Hernandez danced from side to side with the mic held in his left hand. He raised his right in a fist. "Let's tell it to the man. Repeat after me with the rhythm. Black and brown, we own the town."

The crowd screamed his words back at him.

"Racist cops can't keep us down."

Seeming accustomed to call and response, the well-churched audience gyrated to the beat as they belted out his message. The state troopers standing at the edge of the gathering eyed the crowd and mumbled into their radios.

"If righteous whites gonna stick around…"

Voices joined that had seemed uncomfortable up to this point. A call for inclusion. Good.

"Testify now. Let me hear your sound. All of you Hill folks ready to be our allies, say yeah."

"Yeah," Joe said half-heartedly.

"You better convince me you ain't spies for the CIA, the FBI, the state troopers…"

Hand on his hips, Hernandez nodded in the direction of the officers at the crowd's periphery. When the crowd booed, Hernandez turned the mic in their direction and scampered across the stage.

"Or CyanoCorp." He slashed his mic through the air like a stiletto through an intended victim's throat. "If you're on our side, testify."

Well, Joe wasn't on CyanoCorp's side. "YEAH!" he screamed.

"Much better, you're beautiful, welcome to Oakland."

Although the day's theme of unity resonated, unfortunately, it didn't include him. But could it? If he came up with a solution to the mess he'd caused?

Daphne finished her lunch and began mushing rice into her hair. Joe took the bowl and wheeled the stroller away from the crowd to hunt for a trash receptacle. Finding one a few dozen yards down the path, he discarded their refuse. An angry voice commanded him to stop.

"What's wrong?" Joe asked.

"You threw Styrofoam plates and plastic forks in the trash. Are you aware the garbage islands in the North Pacific are now bigger than Alaska and Texas put together?" A young black man in a Cal T-shirt tucked into a pair of chinos postured beside Joe. His tennis shoes appeared new.

Joe rolled his eyes. "What material does the Filipino child labor use to make those sneakers? Have they replaced plastic with children's flesh?"

"Made right here in Oakland by a co-op on Martin Luther King Boulevard. From biodegradable plastics manufactured in contained bioreactors. When they wear out, they'll go in the burn pile to provide clean energy. Any other questions, asshole?"

Shoulders slumped, Joe reverted to his stock refrain. "Sorry."

From behind Joe, a teenage black kid in a football jersey that stretched across bulging biceps burst in. "Leave him alone, schoolboy."

The environmental activist dude backpedaled, taking cover behind a display table. His move exposed a twenty-something blonde.

"That your girlfriend? Some defender you are, kid. Hey Blondie, next time you come to Oakland, bring protection who don't wear ballet slippers."

The woman stepped out in front of the table. "I'm *his*

protection—a black belt in karate. If you come one step closer to my friend, you'll be singing soprano and defecating into a bag for the rest of your life."

Cowed, the kid backed away.

"All talk," she said. "Anyway, as my colleague was saying, responsible citizens avoid petroleum-based plastics. Would you like to see some of our literature?"

Refusal didn't seem to be an option. "Please."

She seized his arm and locked it in a metal tube. Porcupine quills attacked Joe's bicep, but only for an instant before the device snapped open and released him.

"Temporary tattoo. It's the URL for our website. The ink will fade by tomorrow morning, so be sure you bookmark the site. Don't you dare print anything—read it online."

"I will." Joe cowered like a frightened rabbit behind his daughter's stroller.

"You can approach the table," the male student said. "She's like the birds on the lake; she doesn't bite unless provoked."

Joe inched the stroller toward them. "Science for the People," the banner proclaimed. "I've never heard of your group."

"Not many people have. By the way, I'm sorry I called you an asshole. I'm Otis, and my warrior cyborg friend is Melanie." He extended his hand. "I'm kidding about the cyborg part."

"Thanks for clarifying." After pumping his hand in the expected fashion, Joe extended the same courtesy to Melanie. "I'm Larry. And this is Daphne."

"Pleased to meet you, Larry," Melanie said.

Daphne reached for Melanie's hair, but the netting stopped her.

"Is your Daddy a scientist?" Melanie amused Daphne with a game of peek-a-boo while waiting for Joe to answer.

Crap. Best to play this one close to the vest. "I'm jobless at present. I'm moving to Eugene. I'll be looking for work up there."

"Sorry to hear it. Lots of people unemployed with the catastrophe. Otis and I are grad students at Cal."

"So, what are you working on?" Joe asked.

"The solution to Genocide Joe's toxin," Melanie said.

Joe bristled, but curiosity won out. "I'm all ears."

"Well," Otis interrupted, "I don't know how much you know about cyanobacteria, but like all bacteria, they can be infected with viruses called bacteriophage." He leaned against the table and crossed one leg over the other. "Stop me if I'm not making sense."

Stopping him was the last thing on Joe's mind. "Go on. I'm a microbiologist."

"Fabulous. I'll talk in shorthand. We've got a lytic phage that's selective for the species of cyanobacteria causing the problem."

Why would this be useful? "Won't killing all the cyanobacteria upset the ecosystem even more?"

Otis beamed. "Precisely where Melanie comes in. I'm the geneticist; she's an engineer. We're collaborating. She's aerosolized my phage, and if we can get access to helicopters, we can spray it on the Bay. The problem cyanos will see it first since they jut out of the water. And the neat trick—"

"Is Otis's. The guy's a genius. He engineered instability. If the phages don't infect cyanos within minutes of hitting the water, they biodegrade."

Hmm. "Have you tested it?"

"Small-scale. A pond in the UC Botanical Gardens. We've been monitoring every day; we use one diagnostic for the toxin gene and another for the phage. None of either—totally clean." Otis's voice rose to a fever pitch.

Brilliant idea—why hadn't Joe thought of it? "I could help

you get your papers published—I know a few editors at the major journals. Solid pubs might help you get grant funding. I'd also be willing to look at the manuscripts and see if I can anticipate any control experiments the journals might ask for." This was the answer—the way to help the people he'd hurt. Joe's spirits soared.

Melanie gritted her teeth and inhaled. "Who are you? Why do you want to help us? Did you work for CyanoCorp?"

With a wave of his hand, Otis cut her off. "Published papers would be a great back-up plan, but we're shooting for a faster way to get helicopters."

"What's progress like?" Joe asked, preferring Otis's topic of discussion.

"Lousy," Melanie said. She scowled at Otis. Her expression said she suspected Joe's secret.

But chose not to share her suspicion with the crowd. "Police won't help; military won't help. They don't want anything to do with us. They said forget it—why risk being the next Genocide Joe?"

As the original Joe, he couldn't fault them for their misgivings.

Daphne worked the crowd, smiling at anyone who would make eye contact.

In a louder voice, Melanie continued. "Technophobia's the problem. Combatting it is why we're here. If we can explain the approach, locals will march on City Hall with us and demand those helicopters."

The crowd had multiplied. They were paying attention.

A wizened gentleman, head covered with toxin sores, approached the table. "You want us black folks to march on City Hall with you two at the lead? Young woman, I've been protesting ever since I marched with Dr. King on Washington.

I was a little boy back then. That one did some good. So far, not so good with Oakland City Hall."

Melanie turned to the man. "What other option do we have?"

"I don't know." The old man shrugged. "It's why I'm here listening to you. But how do I know you're not another sham? You're going to solve a technology mess with more technology? Let's just say I'm skeptical. And I'm careful who I trust these days. You see the cane I'm walking with? Yeah, I'm old, but I didn't need one until I got beaten. Now I got a bum leg and a bad back. Policeman's club also hit my head—the injury left me real sensitive to the toxin. I'm going to die because of my protesting, so I need to make sure my next cause is worth the time I have left. Convince me."

The crowd went back to chatting or checking their cell phones.

"What do you want to know?" Otis asked.

His gaze locked with Otis's. "You ever been to a sit-in?"

"I haven't."

"A teach-in, then? Or defended a barricade?"

"No." Otis frowned and lowered his head.

"So, you're just some grad students the authorities are ignoring, and you expect to lead us with no experience whatsoever in fighting them?"

Melanie shuffled her feet and responded in a toneless voice. "You make us sound like idiots."

"Well," the old man said, "at least you're here. It's a start. I can introduce you to a few folks you'll want to meet. Right over there, for example..."

Where the man gestured, state troopers were massing. Riot shields in one hand, clubs in the other. Guns in their belt holsters.

"Got to go," the man said. "Nice meeting you." He swung from side to side: cane first, body next. The cops were quicker.

"Where you going, you troublemaker?" Using his riot shield, a state trooper blocked the man's egress. The old man lifted his arms to protect his head as the officer raised his club into strike position. "None of you folks listen to him—he's a radical."

Otis pirouetted between the officer and the old man. "Sir, he's not a threat to you. Please let him go."

"Get out of my way." The cop rapped his shield with his club.

Showing no fear, Melanie pushed her way toward the officer. "Leave my friend alone."

Through his visor, the policeman leered. "White trash here for chocolate, eh?" He hovered over her menacingly.

"Don't you talk to her like that," a matron in church clothes said.

"Shut up, woman."

At this moment, something lobbed from behind the forward line of police exploded with a bright flash and a loud bang. The old lady screamed; young men fled. One jostled her, and she tumbled to the ground.

"Help her," someone shouted. Part of the crowd shuffled toward the woman, part toward the police. More than one hand reached deep in a pocket.

Joe's heartbeat raced. He searched for an opening in the crowd, a way to flee. Fruitlessly. Festivalgoers swirled around them.

Hands emerged from pockets, clasping metal.

"Officers in trouble," a policeman barked into his radio. "We're going in."

Chapter Five

The mob screamed as clubs beat upon flesh. Joe chose a direction and ran, head down, pushing the stroller as fast as he could. The stroller cut through the crowd. Gold chains and pistols headed the opposite way, toward the fight, pausing only to avoid Daphne's carriage.

Confused festival refugees massed on Grand. *"Out of my way!"* Joe shouted. One man glommed onto the stroller. When Joe lunged, the guy's face met Joe's fist. Before he could recover and hit back, Joe raced off.

Daphne made her motorcycle-imitation noise.

They weren't on Grand. Where the hell were they? A street sign. Twenty-seventh. Where that hit Broadway, a walkway passed in front of a restaurant where he'd had lunch a few times. It bridged the distance to Webster Street. He could get most of the way to the MacArthur BART station on Webster.

A good plan, but Twenty-seventh was deserted, and so was his cut-through to Webster. Something wasn't right. Where were the people? "We'll be okay, Daphne." he panted. "Just out for a run."

Joe didn't get far on Webster, only up to the old Alta Bates Medical Center. The hospital was now a military outpost: command and control center for the Oakland National Guard unit.

From the roof, a bullhorn blared: "You, with the baby, stop where you are. Nobody passes."

"You don't understand." Joe's hands pushed against his knees; he forced his head up. Shallow breaths raked his lungs. "My kid... There's a riot."

"We know. You aren't going to pass. The riot stays in the center city. Come any closer, and we'll shoot."

Sweat streamed under Joe's headshield. The view window fogged, so he took it off.

"We don't care that you're white. You radicals are danger-ous. Despicable dragging a baby into this."

"We came to visit the birds," Joe said.

"Not buying it. Turn around, or you're target practice."

Joe relented and turned back. Wheezing, limbs heavy, a sour taste in his mouth, he pressed on, going the wrong way on Webster.

An idea came. An alternative route: Thirtieth was ahead. It hit Telegraph; Telegraph crossed Fortieth; Fortieth ran right into the station.

Toxin be damned, Joe threw Vishva's headshield into the pouch on the back of the stroller. Too exhausted to run, he jogged. He peeked at Daphne. She slept. Good.

At Telegraph, they joined the human migration. The crowd straddled the street and moved en masse. Joe was one more elephant tramping the understory—no way to stop.

But they did. Why? Bodies crushed in. Confusion reigned. Screams. *Help me* cried in four different languages; profanity shouted in at least that many. Pushed, Joe took an elbow to the face. *My child*, someone sobbed.

My child! Joe detached the toxin net from the stroller and nabbed Daphne, wrapping it around her. The stroller was crushed underfoot. Tired, trusting her dad, Daphne pressed her face against his shoulder.

Then, Joe saw. From above on the MacArthur Freeway, National Guard troops dropped teargas canisters onto Telegraph. Snipers fired into the crowd.

To protect Daphne, Joe positioned her like a football. As she fidgeted, the quarterback held her tight and dashed up the middle. First bridge, second bridge, third. Fumes from burning gas closed Joe's throat. Couldn't breathe. He sprinted. Fourth bridge. Eyes grew bleary. A canister exploded. Blazing trash barrels blocked him. He dodged. Again, up ahead, he swerved left.

Eyes closed, he charged. Daphne's breath warmed his arm.

The sound faded. When Joe opened his eyes, he found himself still on Telegraph, but north of the bridge.

He slung Daphne over his shoulder. Sleeping—how? In spite of the tear gas? Oh yes, the netting blocked most air pollutants.

Left on Fortieth. Deserted—maybe it was safe.

Unable even to jog, he shuffled. Straight shot to the station, he persevered. It was calm, quiet. Surreal.

Once there, Joe extracted a credit card from his pocket and purchased a ticket. The machine vended. Spent, he trudged up the stairs.

Joe unbuckled his backpack. With Daphne on his right shoulder, he freed his left arm and collapsed onto a bench. He repositioned Daphne, reclined, and closed his eyes. The train would come eventually.

For a moment, back with Otis and Melanie, he'd had hope,

but the riot had obliterated it. He'd killed the Bay. He'd nearly killed the birds. He'd destroyed this community.

To these people, he was Genocide Joe: epitome of all things evil. Corporate tool. Discarded, useless, broken tool. If he had one shred of dignity left, he'd have leaped in front of the train. Or maybe a train in Oregon, once Daphne was safe with her cousins. It would spare the world any more harm.

"Hey." A voice beckoned. Out of sheer exhaustion, Joe ignored it.

"Hello there," the female voice called out. "I'll come over to your side of the tracks."

When Joe opened his eyes, although tear gas, sweat, and fatigue clouded his vision, he spied the woman he'd met earlier, Sunshine, as she disappeared down the outbound platform staircase. Moments later, she re-emerged near him.

He should pretend to be human and show concern. "Did you and your partner get out all right?"

She froze, bit her lip, appeared to fight back a wave of emotion. "She's angry with me and not coming home. I didn't want to go break windows. She called me a bourgeois sell-out because I wouldn't 'show solidarity' with the Lowlanders against the corporations and the police. Instead, I let a cop escort me out of the area. My white skin and clipboards made me look nonthreatening." Sunshine dropped her gym bag on the pavement and sat opposite him.

"Are you?"

"Nonthreatening to the powers that be? I guess. Nobody wanted to register. Voting didn't seem relevant."

It wasn't what Joe had intended to ask. A gash on her arm concerned him, but her answer indicated the day's primary wounding was psychological.

A large bird with a black head and a white 'chinstrap' waddled toward them.

"Ignore it," Sunshine said. "It's looking for a handout. Idiots feed the Canada geese, and they get aggressive. I'm not fond of them—they shit all over everything and poison the water with their bacteria. Kind of like someone else I know, *Larry*." She sneered when pronouncing his alias. "I know who you are. Some kids told me Genocide Joe had been sighted, and I Googled to find your picture."

Lovely. "So why are you still talking to me?"

Another Canada goose swooped down and perched on top of the information monitor. "Oakland's home for some of the geese. Others migrate." Sunshine shifted position to confront Joe face-to-face. "This is my home. You said you're moving away." She sat up straight and sneered. "I saw you with your daughter—" Sunshine stole a furtive glimpse at the sleeping child, "so I know you're capable of love. The Peace Festival was supposed to be about love. How do you have so much hate that you can destroy my home and then leave? Seriously—I want to know your answer."

It was a fair question. "I heard a great idea today from a couple of grad students—a way to get rid of the toxin. The science is working; what's needed is funding. And community support, but because of my past, the best I can do on this front is disappear. Funding—I can help with. I know people who could pry money out of environmental foundations, enough to get the project off the ground. I'm going to make the connections and then start over."

"More engineering cyanobacteria? Oregon's got a coastline and estuaries to ruin?"

He deserved the rebuke. "Unlikely." But what could he do? "How about you—you seem down on voter registration."

"If I don't keep doing it, who will?"

Vishva would have said Sunshine had found her dharma. And his? "We all contribute how we can, using the skills we have. I don't know what the environmental issues are in Oregon. I'm going to have to do a lot of listening when I get there."

The monitor, which had been blank, blinked on. Outbound train in five minutes; inbound in ten.

"Listening to companies to see what will make them money?" Sunshine asked.

"Been there, done that." Joe had trained to study problems and solve them, but if he'd learned anything today, it was that he needed to be part of a community to determine which problems mattered.

"Is this a promise?"

She'd miss her train if she didn't get over to the other platform. Did he mean what he was saying? As he'd told Kiara earlier, he wasn't a good liar.

He was a decent thief—he'd steal Melanie and Otis' slogan, "Science for the people." Too bland, not enough to claim status as—what was Kiara's phrase? Oh yeah, a *righteous white dude*. He drew on his life experience to add a few heartfelt words. "Fuck the corporations!"

Sunshine fist-bumped him and dashed over in time to catch her train.

Warmth radiated throughout Joe's body. As one of the birds took flight, Joe tipped his head to the sky, his gaze following it toward the horizon, and laughed out loud.

Still inside her anti-toxin cocoon, Daphne awoke and squirmed. Then she noticed the geese. "Birds."

What should he tell her? He bit his lip, pondered. "Your daddy will help clean up their home, so they'll always be there for you." And some will migrate North in the spring to visit, but that was a little much to convey to an eighteen-month-old.

These migratory birds would return to the Bay Area. Like them, he should, too, but also like them, not right away. After

Melanie and Otis's strategy had rid the region of his toxin. When he could come home under his own name and advocate responsible water usage rather than risky tech. *No More Genocide Joes* could be the slogan that saves the Bay.

The slogan that saves him. He could do this. Not as a false white savior, but as partner to those he'd wronged.

Daphne looked him in the eye, reached for him. With a tug, Joe released her from the net and brought her to his shoulder. She gave him a kiss.

"Love you, Daddy." She wrapped her arms around his neck.

He'd do his best to be worthy of that love. When Joe returned the hug, his tear wet Daphne's shoulder. She didn't seem to mind.

With a sound like a wolf's howl, a train whooshed into being. Joe forced himself to a standing position, aided by the rush of air. The train slowed and stopped, the beast quieting, although the magnetic levitation system continued to growl until the doors reached platform height and opened.

"Train," Daphne said. She pushed back to where she could look Joe in the eye.

In those eyes, Joe saw the love Sunshine had assured him he was capable of returning. "Train," Joe replied. *Train, lead us to our new life, so I can help repair the damage I've done with the old one.*

As if in response, the howling started up again.

With his free hand, Joe retrieved the backpack. "You and I will help our friends save the world, kiddo."

She smiled.

Epilogue

Three months later

Joe hadn't wanted to return to Oakland so soon, but the money folks wouldn't have trusted Melanie and Otis's data without the visit. To them, only real-time video would prove authenticity. Everything else could be a deepfake.

He and Otis set out to establish chain-of-custody over a sample using Joe's cell phone. Joe first caught the sign indicating he stood on Lakeside Drive and then fiddled with the settings until he could capture a 360-degree pan of the site. These images would establish for anyone watching later that it was indeed Lake Merritt. Next, Joe switched the camera to selfie mode. The money folks would accept the shot as proof it was Joe wielding the camera.

Once Joe had switched the camera direction back, he nodded to Otis, who took a bottle from his bag, got down on hands and knees, and sampled the water. Otis filled a microfuge tube with an aliquot and marked the tube with the

GPS coordinates. He then froze the aliquot in liquid nitrogen, dumped the rest of the sample back into Lake Merritt, and rinsed the bottle three times. Otis moved twenty meters and repeated these steps at four additional sites around Lake Merritt.

Joe resisted the temptation to sneak glances behind his back. He'd come undisguised. Otis had convinced him Vishva's face shield would have elicited suspicion. Stomach tight as a rock, Joe shivered involuntarily.

With his camera running, Joe followed Otis to the state-certified water testing lab across the street from the UC Berkeley campus. A twentysomething in a T-shirt called from behind the counter. "Hey, Otis. You coming to my party next weekend?"

"Wouldn't miss it." Otis handed her the dewar flask containing the five frozen samples.

"Who's your friend," she asked, turning to Joe.

They hadn't rehearsed this part, so Joe jumped in before Otis could respond. It had only been three months since he'd left the Bay Area—too soon to risk recognition. "The money guy." He was more of an intermediary lining up financiers, but the white lie kept things simple and achieved the desired purpose: as expected, the young woman found him boring and did not further inquire.

After Joe shut his cell phone off and stashed it in his pocket, he and Otis stepped out onto the busy sidewalk. "I've got to get going. Time here is dangerous." He'd driven from Eugene to Sacramento the night before, staying with a friend rather than at a hotel, so no record of his credit card use would exist. Joe would do the reverse trip in the morning.

Otis pivoted toward the opposite direction and headed back to his lab.

* * *

That fall, they met again online. "Can you see and hear me?" Joe asked.

"Yep," Otis said. "And thank you. You came through big time."

Leaning back in his ergonomic chair, Joe pivoted to make eye contact as best as Zoom would allow. "You two solved the science issues. All you needed was money, and I could swing that. Do you have enough helicopters to get going?"

Melanie nodded. "We'll start with Lake Merritt and move on to other parts of urban Oakland. When it works—and it will —we'll have the people and machinery behind us to fix the whole Bay at once. There will be hundreds of copters."

"I'd suggest keeping my name quiet. I'm toxic." It hurt to say this, but it was the truth. "I gave you the names of everyone who donated. None of them will mind getting credit. Let the press focus on them."

"Sounds like a plan," Melanie said.

"Phase B should then start. Write it all up. You've got data; you need pubs. I can help in any way you want. Bounce ideas off of me; let me chase down obscure citations. I'm in Eugene. I can walk to the U. of Oregon library. I'm not recognized as often here. By the time you need a letter for a postdoc position, my name will be cleared, at least with scientists. I can arrange any introduction you'll need."

Pausing, biting his lip, Otis commanded the screen visually, albeit wordlessly. When he did speak, it came out as a forced mumble: "For someone painted as a monster, you've been a godsend."

Joe calibrated his response to inspire a young person. "Corporations will paint you whatever way they want. Don't do corporate. The planet needs you both as professors."

"I like that goal," Melanie said.

"One more thing: I'm planning a get-together in Eugene for next Memorial Day Weekend. Would you two be able to drive up? You can stay with me."

Otis answered for the pair: "It sounds terrific; we'll be there, right, Melanie?"

Following a moment's hesitation, glaring at Otis the entire time, Melanie ultimately nodded. Perhaps Melanie recognized a distinction between a gay, black intellectual making decisions for her and a more unambiguous agent of the patriarchy compelling submission. Or maybe she was just tired. It seemed unwise to pry. "Wonderful. I'll be watching the helicopters on your Discord channel." Once they left the Zoom meeting, Joe powered down his computer.

*** * ***

Eight months later

Joe gazed across the breakfast table at Daphne. The morning before the gathering, Daphne was two years and eight months old. She told everyone who asked: not merely two and a half; rather, two years and eight months. Joe had said lots of friends were coming to stay, and Daphne was over the moon about it.

Unfortunately, Adam wouldn't be there. Joe had found his obituary online. A heart attack, not related to the toxin. Adam would have said he was joining Trudy. If it gave an old man peace, who was Joe to criticize?

Vishva Ray would be coming. He'd organize the Ultimate Frisbee, just like he'd promised. And his wife was bringing her lentil soup.

Melanie, Otis, and both of their boyfriends were driving up. There would be a fifth in their car, but Joe hadn't pried.

Sunshine Love and her partner, Hannah, would come, too. She'd found him through the U. of O. email address adjunct status bestowed. Joe couldn't wait to meet Hannah. She seemed special.

He was a teacher now, a valid use of his skills, but Joe had never dreamed how much he would love it. His microbiology class gave him the top ratings of any instructor U. of O. had, adjunct or tenure track. When the department asked him to also pick up cell biology, he'd acquiesced.

It was an in: faculty would talk with him. He had a lot to learn about Oregon's environment before he could be useful. He took notes on discussions; they would send him papers to read.

Grandma's Barbecue now had a website, so Joe sat at his kitchen table and pecked at his computer, ordering off of it. High-speed rail from the Bay Area meant a piece of Oakland could go this far and taste like delivery to Berkeley. Daphne would finally taste their sweet potato pie. Joe would make all the veggie food and side dishes himself and shop for craft beers.

He stretched and suppressed a yawn as Daphne bounded in to greet him. "Hey, Daphne. How would you like to hit Saturday Market before our friends arrive?"

"Daddy—really?" She put her hands on her hips like her mother used to do. "I love Saturday Market."

Part of Joe wanted to spoil her. She wouldn't let him. Anytime he showed her a dress, she steered him to tie-dyes and jeans. She did like earrings. When she'd told Sunshine hers were pretty, she'd meant it.

Abruptly, Daphne wrinkled her nose and stared at the sky: an "I'm thinking" modality she'd copped from her dad. Then she asked, "What do you call a *special* person even if they're not your cousin for *real*?"

Joe suppressed a chuckle. "An adult can be aunt or auntie. Uncle if a man. Or just their name."

"I have lots of aunties and uncles coming today, right?"

"Yes." And she'd make them all feel special.

By noon, they were back to finish preparations. The first car arrived at two. A candy-apple-red Great Wall Motor R15—the electric vehicle fabricated with the fewest toxic materials, according to an article Joe had read recently—kicked up dust as it traversed the dirt road up to the house Joe had rented. Melanie, Otis, and their plus-ones ambled out.

Kiara was their plus-two.

Joe's knees grew weak, and a breath caught in his throat, but as soon as Otis spoke Kiara's name and mentioned that Kiara loved birds, pointing to the ones in front of him, Daphne rescued Joe from the awkwardness. "I have an auntie who loves birds! Can I show you my favorites?" She offered her hand.

"I would love that." Kiara allowed Daphne to lead her to the lake.

Joe stared in amazement at Otis, "How in the world—"

"It's her story," Melanie said. "She gets to tell it."

Okay.

* * *

Joe whipped up a curry for the seven of them. He made two batches—one goat, and one tofu—an appetizer to hold the crowd over until the barbecue arrived. Nobody other than Hannah wanted tofu, so it went into the refrigerator to be eaten as leftovers.

Just after dusk, Daphne led Kiara home. "Auntie Kiara loved the birds on the Lake."

In response, Joe gestured toward a framed print. "Lake

Merritt Estuary—your favorite place in Oakland? Your auntie came with us one day."

A grin stretched across Daphne's visage. "You did?" She slowed her bouncing by grabbing onto the sofa.

With eyes glued to Daphne's and a serious expression, Kiara nodded.

Bouncing resumed. "That's cool! Can we do it again?"

"Absolutely."

When Daphne got distracted and went to play with Aunt Melanie, Kiara turned to Joe. "You probably have questions."

"Whatever you want to answer, whenever."

"Okay, how about these answers for tonight." Kiara sat beside Joe on the couch. "I know Otis because I now work for him. There were no preschool jobs, and I'm finding making media for bacterial growth fun. It paid more than daycare, and I'm good at it. He's teaching me everything I need to be a tech in a microbiology lab. I asked him if I could come, and he said yes."

Without hesitating, Otis interrupted Kiara: "She's spectacular."

"As is he," Kiara said, also without pausing for breath. "He gives me articles to read and steals time from his day to discuss them with me." Her eyes said thank you to Otis; then, she paused for a moment.

"I've focused, in part, on horizontal evolution. It caused my daughter Imani's death; you didn't. I need until tomorrow to see if you've earned 'righteous white dude' status, but I can talk to you and not think of her, even though I miss her terribly."

Obviating any response from Joe, Daphne arrived atop Melanie's shoulders. She dove into a monkey-like half-jump, landing on the couch next to Kiara and giving her a hug around the shoulders and a kiss on the cheek.

"Everyone's hungry," Kiara said. "More tomorrow. The curry smells delicious—lots of ginger and coriander in the air."

This pleased Daphne, who bounded toward the kitchen. "Mmm. Daddy makes great goat."

The group ate, streamed an old Alfred Hitchcock movie while Joe cleaned up, and settled in for bed.

* * *

Sunshine and her partner arrived the following morning. Other than Joe, only Vishva—who'd arrived late the previous evening —was awake, so he wandered out onto the porch to greet them. "Hello, friends of Joe, now friends of mine. I am Vishva—Joe's technician from CyanoCorp."

His statement evoked an angry growl from Sunshine. "You still work for them?"

"I would rather eat poison."

His response returned a reluctant smile to her face.

Sensing a need to further defuse the situation, Joe poked his head out the screen door to draw their attention. "Pancakes?"

It worked.

With this loquacious a crowd, breakfast lasted two hours. When the grandfather clock Joe had acquired three weeks earlier at Saturday Market struck eleven, Vishva leapt up. "Joe, let's get the Ultimate Frisbee game going."

Awesome. Joe had been looking forward to it. "Sounds good to me."

"Let us go, my friends, old and new." Vishva bounded up without even remembering to put on his shoes. "You must meet me on the grassy area behind where we parked our cars."

As soon as the others lumbered out the door, Vishva took command. Standing barefoot on the grass on Joe's lawn, Vishva picked Otis and Melanie as team captains. Otis's team got Melanie's boyfriend, Hannah, Joe, and Vishva. Melanie's consisted of Vishva's wife, Sunshine, Otis's boyfriend, and Daphne.

Daphne made the winning catch. Held aloft by Sunshine, she snatched the frisbee from the air. Otis's throw was perfect; it sailed right to her. After everyone clapped, Daphne took a bow. Joe had raised a showoff, but an adorable one who could get away with it.

Nonetheless, the game tired her out. Kiara slung the sleepy child over her shoulder and followed Joe as they walked Daphne back for a nap. "I haven't just been working; I've also been taking biology classes." Kiara shifted Daphne to the other shoulder. "I want to go to grad school, and I need a letter of recommendation. Will you write one for me? I figure with you, Otis, and a teacher or two who thought I did well in their classes, I'd have that base covered."

This, he could do, and more. "You'll not only get a letter, but I know lots of people at Cal. Which program are you looking at?"

"Integrative Biology. I want to study evolution." Her hands trembled.

"I'll find out who's on the committee and call them on your behalf."

Kiara beamed. "Thank you." Then, she changed the subject. "So, what are *you* doing here?"

"Teaching. Enjoying seeing my daughter grow up among family who love her." Joe paused as a pair of robins took flight. "And learning about local environmental issues from colleagues as well as activists. I need to know where my skills fit to be helpful. I'm never genetically engineering algae again, but I could probably produce data to guide conservation efforts."

"That sounds like 'righteous white dude' status to me."

Was it? "I try my best."

"It's all any of us can do. I'm looking forward to seeing what you chose for craft beer—I love the stuff."

Later in the evening, as a log burned in Joe's fireplace, they all partook. Eugene rivaled Berkeley for the quality of its alcohol. The room smelled yeasty, with notes from several different fruits. Oddly, Sunshine hadn't tried any of it. Then, Joe noticed her belly.

"You got it, Joe. I'm pregnant. You inspired much nagging, and eventually, Hannah acquiesced. I'll soon be a mom. I can only hope my kid is as wonderful as yours."

Upon hearing this news, Daphne turned and stared at Sunshine. "You're going to be Mommy Sunshine?" Daphne asked.

"Pretty much."

Daphne's grin stretched from ear to ear. "I think you'll be great."

Kiara chimed in. "I agree. And Daphne, you have the best daddy ever. He took you to say goodbye to the birds you loved and brought you to a place with even more." Kiara pointed toward the window.

And Daphne bolted out the door. Not that she'd see birds in the dark, but sensing Daphne's enthusiasm, Otis chased after and took Daphne's hand. The door slammed shut behind them.

Kiara continued speaking to Joe once Daphne and Otis had traveled out of earshot. "Then, you got her through a riot zone with everyone shooting at you, including the racist white cops they brought in to control black people. You knew they were looking at you the same as at me—they didn't give a shit that you were white. Yet, you managed to bring her to Oregon to grow up as part of an extended family."

"Joe?" Vishva asked. "How about Labor Day at my place? Are you ready to come back and see Lake Merritt again?"

He was.

"Mine will be little," Sunshine said. "But not too young to play with Daphne."

"I can't wait," Joe said. It would be terrific to see everyone again. "And there will also be a Cal grad student I'll want to visit." Joe winked at Kiara, and she smiled.

To the world, he'd no longer be Genocide Joe, the murderer, the monster who destroyed the Bay—just a dad taking his daughter on a visit to Lake Merritt—a 'righteous white dude' out to do whatever he could to make the world a better place.

The Personal Odyssey that Led
to This Story

Nail the landing and get out gracefully and quickly is the advice for short story writers who want to sell their work. You don't get to write an epilogue like a novelist does.

I was writing one anyway. I had to find out what happened to my characters, just to satisfy my own curiosity. The plan was to give it away for free on my website. Readers of "The Day We Said Goodbye to the Birds" who, like me, wanted to see what happened to Joe and all the other characters would get to do so. If I was giving it away for free, an epilogue could be a literary fiction vignette rather than the "complete" story most science fiction editors expect. No one would get to wave the "short story rules" in my face.

And if you hadn't wanted to read an epilogue or material explaining the story's origin, so be it. Both were heading to my website, so if I wanted to write them, I would. I never imagined an editor asking for such things.

Why did I care so much? "The Day We Said Goodbye to the Birds" is two-thirds autobiography. I'm Joe. Nice to meet you.

The Personal Odyssey that Led to This Story

My daughter and I did take a trip to say goodbye to the birds at Lake Merritt before leaving the Bay Area. My family was also present at the 1995 Oakland Festival, which broke out into violence in much the same way it did in the story. With my own eyes, I witnessed a white cop brought in from outside the area begin clubbing an old man who walked with a cane and who wasn't moving fast enough for him. Young black men jumped off of a bus to help the elderly gentlemen. A bloodbath ensued. The newspapers and TV blamed black people.

But neither of these two stories were science fiction. They were literary fiction. Who was going to buy literary fiction from me?

I resolved that I would write a hard SF story to link the two literary vignettes. Allan became Joe. I had done molecular biology; I had worked with cyanobacteria. I had collaborated with engineers; I had done water sampling for an environmental science project. I hadn't worked in corporate America, but I had collaborated extensively with corporate scientists. I could have done every bit of the science described in this story.

Now that the story was proper science fiction, who could I sell it to? Bruce Bethke was the editor who had bought the sixth story I ever wrote. He told me back in 2013 that he'd plucked it from the pile when he saw Ph.D. rather than M.F.A. in the cover letter. And sure, the sale was in 2013 and publication wasn't until 2023, but I knew the issues had nothing to do with the story ("Caliban's Cameras," which ran in **Stupefying Stories** Volume 25). Bruce had, at the point I submitted "The Day We Said Goodbye to the Birds," published three other stories from me: two flash pieces on the Stupefying Stories website ("Mother Noodges Best" and "Clinical Progress of Witness Deprotection Client L.M. as Transcribed from Taped Recordings") and another that ran in

Volume 26 of **Stupefying Stories** ("Midnight Meal at a Kobe Noodle Joint").

He has since bought two additional stories. I'm calling "Power and Control Through Vocabulary" character-driven hard SF (a phrase I'm sure I invented). It narrowly missed selling as horror, cyberpunk, and heaven help me, literary fiction, again and again. It will run in *Stupefying Stories* Volume 27.

I had a difficult time selling it. I faced rejection after rejection.

Why so much trouble? It was because the protagonist isn't classically likable. Oh, he's likable, but he's a sociopath who tricks you, brave reader, into siding with him and empathizing. And it's a romance. And she's a sociopath too.

In most cases, it never emerged from slush. Slushers are told at most venues to reject by the first page if the story didn't conform to "the rules." Once in a blue moon, it would reach an editor's desk. Numerous personal rejections told me no editor would have the confidence to run a story with a protagonist like mine. They all feared their readers couldn't be subjected to him.

News flash, folks—readers are far less conservative in their tastes than editors think. This conservatism combined with the length (~7000 words) led to rejection after rejection.

Until I sent it to Bruce. He bought it immediately, despite slush submissions being closed. He doesn't care about "the rules." That's incredibly rare among editors.

Bruce has also purchased a reprint that will run in Volume 28: "Salvation Sellers Last Customer." It has been out of print since fictionmagazines.com collapsed; the original publication was in their science fiction imprint, *Nebula Rift*, on a royalties-only basis. I never received a dime.

This one is equal parts cyberpunk and humor. It is the only

time I've ever slowed down my production of new content to try to sell a reprint, but I needed to see this story accessible to the world. I thought it one of my best, but it was the wrong length (a novelette); a reprint from an obscure and extinct venue; and an odd combination of cyberpunk with humor. Who would buy it?

Bruce Bethke, whose first novel also combined cyberpunk with humor. Not that I knew this at the time, but I have since read *Headcrash* and thoroughly enjoyed it. This early cyberpunk classic stands up, even thirty years later.

Maybe Bruce's process isn't the fastest, but the time window is definitely way down. Time from initial submission to acceptance on his latest purchase, "Glossary of Terms Used from Monograph on Human Culture during the Period of Conquest, Kindle Edition," another for the *Stupefying Stories* website, was well under a year.

Regardless, from 2013 on, I could claim an editor whose name you could find in Wikipedia had bought a story from me. Do you recognize the name Bruce Bethke? How about the title of Bruce's 1983 story: "Cyberpunk?" Yes, 1983—a year before *Neuromancer*. I could brag about that sale in cover letters for submissions until I had pro-rate sales.

I trusted Bruce. Holding a story from me did not signify doubt in my story. If he didn't like one, it would have been an honest, quick "no." But that has never happened.

Submission of "The Day We Said Goodbye to the Birds" was direct. I described the story in an email, and Bruce said go ahead and send it. Slush submissions were closed to the rest of the planet. He bought it.

Anyway, Bruce liked "The Day We Said Goodbye to the Birds" but had one very important editorial comment: it was too intense to run without breaking the story into chapters. Chapters would allow an epilogue. He also wanted an essay on how the story came to be. Both of my passion projects would see publication, and not just on my website.

As for his one other request, an essay about the science underlying the story? Easy.

This, dear reader, is offered to you as my final supplement to "The Day We Said Goodbye to the Birds." Enjoy.

The Science Behind the Story

The last thing I promised Bruce was that I'd elaborate about the science. The key to this story is understanding what horizontal evolution is.

Vertical evolution, people have heard of. Favorable variations passed on, selective advantages, eventually optimizing a trait; what Darwin said. It's why you share more genes with a lemur than with a fish.

But it isn't the way microbes evolve. It couldn't be—it's too slow. Yes, over billions of years, you can generate microbes that can live in any niche through vertical evolution alone. It doesn't explain why pesticide resistance will rise in a single farmer's field over a summer to the point that the pesticide can't be used again. It doesn't explain variants of COVID-19 arising in a single, elderly, anti-vax patient who is just strong enough to seed the next phase of the pandemic before COVID kills him. (Okay, I'm employing a gendered stereotype here, but you bought it that it was a guy. He likely lives in Florida.)

In microbes, non-Darwinian evolution predominates, especially in viruses and bacteria. The key is getting foreign DNA into a bacterial cell (or genome) or into a viral genome. With bacteria (as in this story), there are three ways: transfection, transduction, and transformation.

Transfection is using something other than a naturally occurring virus (a virus of a bacterium is called a bacteriophage) to get nucleic acid into a cell. Most of the people reading this have had it done to them. The BioNTech/Pfizer and the US National Institute of Allergy and Infectious Diseases (NIAID, headed from 1984 – 2022 by Anthony Fauci)/Moderna vaccines against COVID-19 are nucleic acid going directly into your cells.

Donald Trump did two things right: he tabbed Anthony Fauci as our country's chief medical advisor and he okayed Project Warp Speed. I don't know for sure, but the strategy of giving out billions of dollars to companies with no obligation to pay anything back was likely Fauci's idea. If so, Trump listened. Not caring that the only other entity capable of doing what his agency did was a German company with the ideas coming from a Turkish immigrant couple—I'll bet Fauci had a hand in that too.

You are not getting a weakened or altered virus when you get these vaccines (the conventional approaches). You are getting stabilized nucleic acid wrapped up in a lipid bubble. That's transfection. It works better with bacteria, but it works just fine with you. My guess is Trump thought if you were making American companies rich (Pfizer and Moderna), if you also happen to make Germans and Turks rich, so be it.

Transduction is when a virus gets in and out of a genome imprecisely and carries a gene along with it. That happens all the time in nature. However, it a lab, it can be made to happen precisely. Scientists splice whatever gene they want into a virus, and the virus gets it into the bacterial genome post-infection.

The scientist's favorite tool for this is phage lambda, one of the earliest characterized bacteriophages. Phage lambda, by the 1990s, was available as two arms that came frozen in test tubes. You combined them with your favorite DNA, mixed with *E. coli* bacterium which had natural sites on the cell membrane for the recombinant phage lambda to attach, and infection occurred.

The whole shebang uses enzymes inside *E. coli* to circularize. A circular piece of DNA carried by a bacterium is called a plasmid. These plasmids can then be recovered, ending up the equivalent of a chemical sitting on a shelf in a lab.

Until the researcher uses our last technique, that is—transformation—to put the plasmid into any other bacterial cell they want. (There are many variants on all of the above—I'm trying to keep things simple.) You recall the resistance to pesticides I mentioned earlier? A gene for transporting copper (copper is a common pesticide) moves as a plasmid, naturally, each summer. It is one form of bacterial sex; the plasmid moves by bacteria mating.

In the lab, there are myriad ways to transform cells. They work. Scientists can put any gene into any well-behaving bacterium in the lab. You can make a pure chemical on a machine (DNA) and easily get it into bacteria. And it's functional, like any other gene.

Scientists are now successful at transforming natural populations in the wild. And here's where in my story, a feasible experiment becomes a disaster and kills much of Oakland. But a caution first. There are some cases where things are so bad that this is a valid and justified strategy.

I live near one such case. Poorly written laws allowed irresponsible pet owners to dump animals they didn't want to deal with—big pythons—into the Everglades. They have eaten 90% of the mammal population. What's left are small rodents that can infect humans with many viruses. The situation is so terrible that even big risks are justified.

There are early-stage genetically engineered products—microbes that kill pythons—being developed. I fully support a genetic-engineering attack on the pythons. There is no other feasible option. And Florida is a good place for this. There's wi-fi in any hotel in Naples or Miami. There is the opportunity for monitoring the science.

The Global South is also watching another project underway in Florida involving field use of genetic engineering: engineering mosquitos to end the spread of Dengue Virus. The issue of having Americans (or British researchers in this case) operating in Florida involves no imperialism. If it works in Florida, Africans can decide to save Africa with proven technology. But it will be an African choice, not a choice imposed upon Africa.

So, where is the hard SF in "The Day We Said Goodbye to the Birds"? A little got told to Adam. Vishva mentioned a bit more. But most got explained to Kiara in the ten minutes when she was deciding whether to let a mob kill Genocide Joe.

Vishva mentioned he was guilty about his part in engineering the cyanobacteria—he overexpressed a gas vesicle gene. Although your high school textbook called bacteria a big bag with chromosomes in the middle; the cell biology of some is fascinating. Gas vesicles are the product of one gene—one type of protein. Okay, maybe a few other types of protein, too, but they play minor roles. When made, the gas vesicle proteins fold up to enclose a space that can fill with air. They cause the bacteria to float. Usually, the regulation is at the step of destroying these vesicles. Enzymes called proteases are made that chew them up. Vishva overexpressed the instructions (a gene) for making gas vesicles, which means the bacteria made a lot of them, so they "jumped out of the water."

So, Joe had cyanobacteria jumping out of the Bay. What else did he put into them? Water channels. Again, your K-12 experience is likely failing you here. Yes, water transport occurs across cell membranes via osmosis, but sometimes it is too slow. Your kidneys have very important water transport that isn't passive osmosis. You'd die without it.

Most water transporters are simple: a hole opens up. Water flows from the less salty side to the saltier side. It is similar to osmosis in that the energy comes from asymmetric distribution of sodium ions, but it proceeds through a watery path, not across a membrane.

However, this couldn't work for Joe, because he needed water vapor to go from the air, condense, and end up in the Bay. He needed a directionality inherent to the pumping. So, he started with bacteriorhodopsin, a protein that uses light energy to pump hydrogen ions out of cells. In nature, it is found with another protein that lets hydrogen ions get back into the cell as a way to take sodium ions out. This exchange allows a microbe called *Halobacterium salinarum* to live in high-salt water. Those pretty colors you see in salt flats from an airplane going into SFO? These are them. To summarize: light leads to pushing hydrogen ions out of the cell, and when they flow back in, sodium ions leave the cells, and thus these bacteria can live in salty water.

Joe started with the bacteriorhodopsin gene, and instead of pumping hydrogen ions, he made it pump water. Water is two hydrogens and an oxygen. With a lot of work and modern computers, making these changes is likely doable.

The next parts are likely also feasible: engineering many of these to stick together and get to the bottom of the cells (not at the air-water interface), so the pushing out of water goes into the Bay. The top of a cell sits in the fog and draws in replacement water from the air.

The molecular biology is feasible. Engineering would come next—could this go at a fast enough rate to make a difference? Talking with engineers, I got three types of answers: maybe, it's a stretch, and consult an engineer when you get the bacteria made. The last answer would have been what Joe would have done. With enough funding, the entire project was plausible.

Then horizontal evolution kicked in. These bacteria picked up a toxin gene and added a lipid that made it volatile. This happens all the time in nature. In my story, a volatile toxin traveled through the air and killed people.

The Bay was dying because of water politics. To obviate politics, CyanoCorp tried science. When they failed, they blamed Joe and let the media crucify him. I find this last part—a corporation denying responsibility with the collusion of government—the most plausible thing I said in this story.

The message here is science is not value-neutral. It could be incredibly important in getting us through the climate catastrophe. It could also be manipulated to create a world where a few billionaires are comfortable and most of the planet experiences a living hell. We have very little time before this transition point will be passed.

In an ideal world we'd have adults as our politicians, willing to decide rationally what the entire world must do. Ahem...

We need Global North scientists and leaders to get us through these crises without killing off the entire Global South and leaving all non-rich occupants of the North in conditions that resemble Haiti or Guatemala today. It's a big ask. But the next generation is in serious trouble if it doesn't happen. And it needs to happen now.

I write to start conversations. There are a lot of conversations that need to happen. I hope my story gets you thinking. And if it takes autobiography to lead you in, so be it.

I hope you enjoyed my story. If you want to see more stories like this one, check out the tabs at allandyenshapiro.com.

About the Author

Allan Dyen-Shapiro is a Ph.D. biochemist currently working as an educator. He's sold stories to numerous markets, including *Flash Fiction Online* (where he is a First Reader), *Dark Matter Magazine*, *Grantville Gazette*, *Small Wonders*, *Factor Four*, *Stupefying Stories*, and many anthologies. You can find his blog and links to his stories at allandyenshapiro.com, or find him on social media at the following links.

- http://www.facebook.com/allandyenshapiro. author
- https://www.goodreads.com/AllanDyen-Shapiro
- http://www.twitter.com/Allan_author_SF
- https://wandering.shop/@Allan_author_SF (Mastodon)

- https://bsky.app/profile/allandyenshapiro.bsky.
  social (Bluesky)